Take Me With You When You Go

by ALAN VENABLE
paintings by LAURIE MARSHALL

ONE MONKEY BOOKS
San Francisco
OneMonkeyBooks.com
2008

For the second grade students of
Chinese American International School,
who first heard this story and gave it meaning.

For the third grade students of Novato Charter School,
who first brought it to life on stage.

And
For a brave, loving, and generous uncle,
Colin Mark Portnuff, 1951-2007.

Published 2008 by
One Monkey Books
156 Diamond Street
San Francisco, California 94114-2414
OneMonkeyBooks.com

Book design by Kristine Brogno

For a teaching guide and school play of this story visit
OneMonkeyBooks.com or email Publisher@OneMonkeyBooks.com.

Library of Congress Control Number: 2007929524

ISBN: 978-0-9777082-7-7

10 9 8 7 6 5 4 3 2 1

Take Me With You

Earth turn, Breeze blow, Brave seeds___ Wind sow.

Take me, With you, With you when you go.

Hear the tune at OneMonkeyBooks.com.

Contents

Sister & Brother Forgotten

Once together, never apart, Brother and Sister came into life. But by the time they could wrinkle their noses, the only one to care for them was a grandmother, on a mountain out at the wild end of the world. She called them Sister and Brother Forgotten.

The granny was old and her shack was small. She was lame and her hands were stiff. All she could do all day was hold Brother and Sister in her lap until they were ready to crawl. Then she let them loose, and they wandered the yard on all fours, finding eggs that the hen had laid and rolling them back to Granny. When Brother and Sister learned how to walk, they began to feed leaves to the goat. Whenever the nanny goat nursed her kid, Brother and Sister would fetch a pot and milk the nanny, too. In ways like these, they began to look after themselves.

In time, all Granny could do was sing them to sleep each night with bits of a tattered old song:

Earth turn
Breeze blow
Brave seeds
Wind sow

Take me
With you
With you when you go

You may wonder how these three—so old and so young—could live by themselves. Well, now and then, a bearded old peddler came by. For a bowl of soup and a place to sleep, he would patch a hole in the roof or mend the spring in the clock.

One evening, he asked Granny, "Who will raise this girl and boy when you are gone?"

"I fear they must raise themselves," she replied.

When Sister and Brother learned to speak, they asked her, "Granny, where do we come from?"

The old woman strained her brain and said, "Suppose you came from apples."

"Then what are apples?" Brother asked. "And where do apples come from?"

"Trees," said Granny.

"Like those?" Sister pointed out at the trees beyond the fence.

"No. There used to be apple trees out there, but now they are gone."

"Where did they go?" asked Brother.

Granny answered sadly, "Gone with my daughter and sons."

One winter morning, the mountain lay covered in snow.

"Granny, are you still asleep?" called Brother. "Get up and build a fire."

"I'm not asleep," she replied. "But I'm too weak to build the fire anymore."

"Teach us to build it, then," he said.

"Very well."

So Granny taught them how to build the fire.

When it was lit, she said, "Sister, Brother, today you must go to my son, your eldest uncle, and send him back to fetch me. Then the three of us can live with him. But be sure he comes before dark, so we don't get lost in the frozen woods."

Brother was worried. He said, "We've never been out alone together beyond the gate."

Granny answered, "When you are together you're never alone. As for daring to go, I know you will. Many times, I've watched your sister climbing your back to reach the latch."

"We'll go," said Sister. She felt that she and Brother had some business out in the world. "How do we find our eldest uncle?"

"Help me out through the snow to the gate," said Granny, "and I will point you the way."

In the deep snow out at the gate, Granny took off her shawl and wrapped it around them both.

"There," she said. "Maybe this will keep you from freezing." Then she opened her hand and showed them something small, withered, and brown. "This was an apple," she said. "I've kept it so long, it's dried up and shrunk. It's all I have left to give you to keep you from starving along the way."

"Could this apple help us find the tree we came from?" Sister asked, tucking the apple into her cap.

Granny replied, "Ah, well, you didn't come straight from apples."

"We didn't?"

"No, you came from a mother and father, as all of us do."

"What's a mother?" Sister asked.

"Well, I was once a mother," said Granny.

"Was the peddler a mother, too?" asked Brother.

Granny smiled. "No," she said. "But winter days are short, and you have far to go. When we see each other again tonight, I will tell you all I know about mothers, fathers, apples, and trees. Now, one more thing. Show me you remember some bit of the song I sing to help you sleep."

"Of course," they replied, and sang,

Earth turn
Breeze blow
Brave seeds
Wind sow

Take me
With you
With you when you go

Granny nodded and said, "From now on, you can sing it whenever you're lonely or sorry or lost."

Granny opened the gate. She pointed down a snowy trail. "Follow this trail off the mountain," she said. "Be brave and stay together, and when you reach your uncle's clearing, don't forget to send him back. Now give me a kiss good-bye."

A sharp wind cut through the winter woods. On frozen branches, crows huddled and shivered and muttered their caws. Below them, Sister and Brother waded through deep snow, singing bits of Granny's song:

Winter
Ice grow
Seeds sleep in
Deep snow

Take me
With you
With you when you go

At midday, the sun hung pale and low. Sister was hungry. She took out the tiny brown apple. She nearly put it in her mouth. Then she felt the shawl stretch out behind her. Brother was dragging behind.

"He must be hungrier than I," she thought, and offered the apple to him.

But Brother said, "No. You're just as hungry. I only drag when I turn to look back where we came from. Eat the apple and fill yourself up, so you'll walk a little slower."

"Slower?" Sister replied. "We need to go faster. You eat it so it will speed you up."

So neither one of them would eat it, and it looked so small that it might disappear if they tried to divide it. Sister put it back in her cap.

Later that day, they came across the peddler, lying in a snowdrift.

"Peddler," asked Sister, "why are you lying out here in the snow?"

"Sister and Brother Forgotten! I haven't eaten in three cold days. Finally, I just lay down and this quilt of snow covered me up."

"Poor peddler, you must eat," said Sister. She took the apple out of her cap.

The peddler sat up and tasted the apple. At first, he tasted nothing, but as a bit of it moistened and sweetened in his mouth, a grin spread across his face. Soon, he had chewed and swallowed the whole thing. Then he stood up, rubbed his stomach, and spat two seeds away.

"So I won't starve after all." he said. "At least, not today. But, Sister and Brother, why are you out so far from home this winter day?"

Said Sister, "Granny sent us to find Eldest Uncle. From now on, we must live with him."

"Your uncle's clearing lies ahead," said the peddler, brushing snow from his beard. "But if I were you, I'd go home to your granny. Your eldest uncle may treat you well, but as for his wife—such a crow! Last time I stopped there hungry, she fed me nothing, and chased me away from her pig trough. If I had any choice...."

"But we have no choice," said Brother, "now that Granny's too old."

"Well," said the peddler, "I've said all I can, but once together and never apart, and better days may come."

So Sister and Brother continued on. The day turned even colder as the sun disappeared behind the mountain, but soon after that, they came to a clearing. As they did, they heard the knock of an axe in the woods.

CHAPTER TWO

Brother & Sister Left-Behind

In the clearing was a cabin with three feet of snow on the
roof. Outside, a woman was taking laundry down from a line,
thinking she could dry it in the winter wind. She was all in
black, and tall and skinny as her laundry poles. She scowled at
Sister and Brother.

"Caw," she said, flapping a sheet.

"Please," said Sister, "we are Sister and Brother Forgotten.
We've come to speak with Eldest Uncle."

The woman pointed a long arm out toward the sound of
the axe.

"Feather-brains! Don't you hear him out there? And what
business could you have with him?"

"Please," said Brother, "Granny can't live alone anymore. She
asks Uncle to come before nightfall and fetch her home to stay."

"And what about you?" the woman asked.

"We must live with you as well."

"Really? And how shall I feed you? I might feed one, but not all three. Tell me which one of you two eats the least."

"Neither of us eats much," said Sister. "After all, we're only children."

"No children of mine," said the woman. She cupped her bony hands to her mouth and shouted, "Husband!"

Her call echoed out through the barren trees. Soon, a tall, thin man walked out of the woods, carrying an axe and a saw.

"These two are Forgottens," said Eldest Aunt. "They say your mother has let herself get too old, and you must go and bring her here."

"Very well," said the man.

"Well, you say?" Aunt flapped her ragged sleeves like wings. "And then what? How am I to feed all three?"

Eldest Uncle looked down at Sister and Brother. He said, "So these are the ones my sister left behind." A tear welled up in his eye. "Are we so short of food?"

"It's them or the pigs," the wife replied.

"As you say, my dear," said Uncle. "But look after them until I get back."

He fetched a lantern and hurried off toward Granny's. When he was gone, Aunt's eyes turned small and sharp.

"So, you two expect to stay?" she said. "Then show me you are good for something. Take down the rest of the wash."

Sister reached up, trying to unpin a frozen pair of overalls. Brother jumped at a sock that hung over the line. But their fingers were numb and they caught the line instead of the clothes.

Down came the line and poles and all the laundry—down on the dirty, trampled snow beneath their feet.

"Feather-brains!" the aunt shouted, picking up the fallen clothes. "Now I must wash this all again! No wonder you were left behind. And, since you have broken the poles, you two can hold up the line yourselves. Pick it up and raise your arms."

The children obeyed. They picked up the icy rope and held it over their heads, though there was not a speck of laundry on it. For an hour they stood there, growing stiff and freezing because the shawl wasn't long enough to cover them both when they stood apart. When the sun disappeared behind the mountain, the aunt came out of the cabin and ordered them to go inside. There, she made them sit in a corner until the uncle returned. Inside, they thought they would be warmer, but the aunt refused to light a fire, so they were nearly as cold in the cabin as they had been standing outside.

Brother shivered and whispered to Sister, "At least Granny will be with us tonight."

"And did you hear what Eldest Aunt called us?" she replied through chattering teeth.

"Yes. She called us Feather-brains."

"True," said Sister, "but she also said that we are Left-Behinds, which means at least we aren't Forgottens."

"Is that much better?" Brother asked.

"It doesn't sound worse," she said.

Brother thought a bit and said, "If we are Left-Behinds and not Forgottens, maybe whoever left us will come back for us again."

"Or we can go looking for them," said Sister. "And did you hear what Eldest Uncle said? He said that his sister left us behind. We must learn more about that."

Brother nodded, adding, "Meanwhile, let's make ourselves useful to Aunt and see if we can warm her heart."

It was dark when Eldest Uncle returned. His lantern lit up the gloomy room.

"Where's the old woman?" asked his wife.

"Gone."

"Gone? Gone where?" she asked.

"Gone and buried," he said.

"Buried?" said Sister and Brother.

"Yes," said Uncle. "She kissed me good-bye and died. I planted her like an old seed, with a pickaxe in the ground."

Brother and Sister Left-Behind cried as though their hearts would break. Who else in the whole, wide world but Granny had ever held them in her lap?

"Stop squawking!" snapped the aunt. She threw Granny's shawl on the fireplace stones. "Lie down and go to sleep."

Then the aunt climbed into bed, complaining to her husband, "What a trick your mother played on us—leaving those two in our nest!"

"Poor Mother," Uncle sighed.

It was hard for Sister and Brother to fall asleep on stones. For a while, they whispered sadly, back and forth, all the good things they remembered of Granny. And of course, she had known it was time to go, so she must have gone in peace. Still, they missed her terribly, shivering under her old, thin shawl.

Only one thought made them feel better: whoever had left them behind years ago might someday find them and take them back.

〜⊙〜

It is hard to say how long they lived with Eldest Uncle and Aunt, for someone like Eldest Aunt makes each day as cold as the last. Each morning, icicles hung from the roof. Each morning, the aunt poked her beak out from under her blankets to order the children up.

"Left-Behinds," she would caw, "get up and build the fire!"

So the children got up and built the fire the way they had learned from Granny. Then Aunt stuck her head out of bed.

"Now punch the ice from the top of the bucket and boil me my bitter-root tea."

That was the next thing she would say. After her tea was boiled, Aunt would get up and throw the children a cold rutabaga for breakfast.

Meanwhile, Eldest Uncle sat up and pulled on his boots. He sharpened his axe, picked up the saw, and said to Brother, "Come."

The two went out in the snowy morning. All day they worked in the woods. First, Uncle would chop down a tree, then say to Brother, "Now saw off the branches and pile them up to make a home for some wild beast. Cut the trunk into pieces and stack them to dry, and scatter the chips and sawdust for hungry mushrooms to eat. You must know that the trees can't do without mushrooms, as mushrooms can't do without trees."

So Brother sawed while Uncle chopped another tree. The work was hard, but it kept them from freezing.

"My boy," Uncle would say at noon, "let us rest while the sun is bright."

From his coat, he took out a cold, boiled rutabaga and shared it, half and half. Brother ate only part of his half. The rest he tucked away in his cap to share with Sister that night, because Aunt never let Sister have lunch.

One midday, Brother asked, "Uncle, what becomes of all this wood we cut down?"

"We sell it for firewood," Uncle replied.

"Is that all these trees are good for?"

"My boy," said Uncle, "there are trees and there are trees. Now, if I came across a fine little apple or cherry tree, I would admire its blossoms in spring, and in summer I'd fatten myself on its fruit."

"Did there used to be such trees?" asked Brother.

"Yes," replied Uncle. "Back when the mountain was strong. Here on the edge of the mountain, these woods were once full of apple trees. That's how things were, years ago, when I courted my wife. And the rich, black earth was full of truffles."

"What are truffles?" Brother asked.

"Truffles!" Eldest Uncle smacked his lips. "Truffles are a sort of mushroom that grows underground by the roots of a tree. To find them, we followed wild pigs that could sniff and snout them out. But now all that is gone, since so many old, good kinds of trees have been cut and taken away. And now, the only pigs that are left are ones that my dear wife raises for pork."

As the days passed, Brother grew used to his life. At least, he always felt useful and Uncle treated him well. But he could not be truly happy because things went so hard for Sister. No matter how much she tried to help Aunt, all she ever got in return were the old crow's caws.

"Scrub the floor with this icy water!" Aunt would say. "Caw!" So Sister scrubbed.

"Now clean the window with vinegar," Aunt would tell her. "And no squawking when the smell of the vinegar burns your nose."

So Sister cleaned and held her nose so it wouldn't sting from the vinegar smell.

"Sweep the snow off the porch! Now grind my bitter roots. Now peel these rutabagas. Now go out and feed the pigs. Caw!"

"Eldest Aunt," said Sister one day, "you don't need to give me so many orders. I've learned what you want me to do. But tomorrow, may I go out to work with Uncle and Brother instead? I am just as strong as Brother."

"No!" The aunt's hair ruffled like long, black feathers. "Then who would I boss around all day? Oh, what a terrible life I lead. I should never have been born as a human. I should have been hatched as a delicate songbird that chirps all day in its nest. Caw! Now scrub the floor again!"

Aunt got meaner and meaner, and Sister's life got worse and worse. Still, there was one time of day when Sister smiled and hummed. That was the hour when Aunt sent her out to feed the pigs. Then, Sister would sing to herself:

Snort, snort
Snouts go
Pig tail
Pig toe

Take me
Pig-gies
With you when you go.

"Take this bucket of peels," Aunt would say, "and dump it in with the pigs. But close the pig shed door behind you, so they can't run away and turn wild."

In the shed lived two grown pigs—a boar and a sow. When Sister arrived with her bucket, the two big pigs would eat at the trough. There were also two piglets that suckled for milk when the sow lay down. Sister loved her pigs. Who wouldn't?

"Family of pigs," she would say, "how happy you must be!"

By and by, the piglets grew bigger and began to eat peels from her hand.

One day she asked the aunt, "What should I call the two piglets?"

"Call them bacon and lard!" snapped the aunt.

"The problem is," said Sister, "I need names to tell the two apart, and I don't know any names at all."

"Caw," replied Aunt. "For the little I care, you can call them Mudworth and Porcabella."

So that's what Sister named the piglets—Mudworth and Porcabella.

But really, Sister did have one other bright moment at the end of every day. That was when Uncle and Brother returned.

~⊙~

One frosty morning, an odd thing happened in the woods. Brother found a tree growing out of season, near the path where the peddler had spit out the seeds.

"What kind of tree is that?" Brother asked.

"Why, that's an apple tree," said Uncle. "It's grown so quickly, it's getting an early start on spring. I can hardly remember the last time I saw a living apple tree."

"Shall we cut it down for firewood?"

"No, let it grow."

Uncle moved on to a different tree. As Brother followed, the apple tree rustled behind him.

"Cut me down!" the tree whispered.

Brother had never heard of a whispering tree. "I must be hearing the wind," he thought.

But after that, whenever he passed nearby, the tree whispered again. Even in his dreams it whispered, "Cut me down."

"What makes you mumble in your sleep?" asked Sister one night.

Brother replied, "It's the apple tree, telling me to cut it down."

"Well," said Sister. "Sneak out tonight and do it."

That night, when Uncle and Aunt were asleep, Brother took the saw and sneaked out barefoot on the snow. A full moon helped him find the tree.

"Saw me down," the apple tree whispered.

So Brother sawed it down.

"Now saw the branches off my trunk."

So Brother sawed off branches until all that was left was a log.

"Hide me under my branches for now," said the log. "But take me with you when you go."

So Brother hid the log.

Next evening, when he and Uncle returned from the woods, Aunt stood in the clearing with Uncle's truffle spade in her hands and the apple log under her boot.

"Look what I found when I went out digging roots for my tea," she said. "A long, straight piece of wood. Husband, split this into laundry poles."

"No, don't split me!" cried the log, but only Brother heard.

"Please, Eldest Aunt," he said, "the log doesn't want to hold up the wash."

"I don't care what it wants!" she replied. "Husband, do as I say!"

But Uncle was tired from working all day. "Let it wait until tomorrow," he said.

"Wait?" she cried. She struck the log with the spade.

"Ouch!" said the log, but only Brother heard.

Uncle frowned at his wife. "My dear," he said firmly, "tomorrow, but not today. Now the boy and I must rest."

That night, as the children lay on their stones, they heard the aunt whisper to Uncle, "Never mind the log tomorrow. I forgot—it's the first day of spring. In the morning send the children into the woods. While they are gone, we shall kill and eat the piglets—one for you and one for me. Caw, how I long to eat pork!"

"We could share with the children," said Uncle.

"Why?" she answered. "They're none of ours. They're Left-Behinds. Just send them out to dig my roots, and so get them out of the house."

"Did you hear that?" Sister whispered to Brother. "We can't let them eat the piglets!"

Now, Brother was not as bold as Sister. Besides, Uncle had shown him love, and Brother could not repay love with a trick. But Brother also loved the piglets and feared for their lives. So, late that night, he and Sister sneaked out to the shed and pulled out the sleeping baby pigs.

At the edge of the woods, they knelt and whispered, "Mudworth, Porcabella, wake up! Run off and be wild!"

The piglets awoke and understood. They squealed and ran off in the dark, and the children sneaked back to the cabin. Later that night, big drops of rain began to fall. Next morning, the rain beat on the roof like a drum.

"Children," said Uncle, "take my truffle spade out in the woods. Go dig your aunt roots for her tea."

"And make sure they're bitter!" warned Aunt.

"Come," said Uncle, "I will show you where to dig."

The children were glad to hear this order. At least it would get them away from the house before the aunt learned what they had done. She would be so angry that, surely, she would want revenge! Wrapped in Granny's shawl, they followed Eldest Uncle out into the pouring rain.

"Uncle, we must tell you the truth," said Brother. "Last night we set the piglets free, and Aunt will soon find out they are gone."

"I thought so," said Uncle. "I heard you go out in the night. Now, I'm afraid you won't be safe here anymore."

"Where can we go?" asked Sister.

"Go to Second Uncle and Aunt, and ask them if they will take you in."

"A second aunt and uncle?" asked Brother. "Where?"

"Take this path down from the clearing," said Uncle. "It will join a muddy trail through the woods. By and by, that muddy trail will widen into a muddy road. And if the road hasn't washed away, it will bring you to a crossroad. You'll find your uncle's sawmill nearby."

The children shouldered the heavy log. It was wet and slippery to hold.

"Uncle," said Sister, "tell us before we go. Is it true your sister left us behind?"

"It's what I believe," he replied. "But sad things happened, and I don't know where she went. Now, leave before your aunt gets up."

The children nodded.

"One more thing," said Uncle. "May I have that old thin shawl? You see, your granny was my mother, and that shawl is all I would have to remember her by."

Sister and Brother looked at each other and nodded. They pulled off the shawl and gave it to Uncle. Then Uncle took off his tattered coat and draped it over them instead.

He said, "Down in one of those pockets, you might find an old double cherry I've kept all these years for luck. It's not much, but it's all I can give you to keep you from starving along the way."

With a tear, he picked up his truffle spade and headed back to the cabin.

Brother and Sister started down the muddy path. They had not gone far when they heard a long, high cry behind them.

"Caaaw!"

What did it mean? It meant that Eldest Aunt had found out her piglets were gone. She stood in the clearing, cawing and flapping like she might take off after Brother and Sister!

"Run!" cried Brother.

And so they did.

It rained as though the storm would wash the earth away. The muddy track down through the woods became a mucky slide. The mud got deeper and deeper until Brother and Sister slipped and fell with every step. Each time they got up out of the mud, they were tempted to leave the log behind. But then the log would tell them, "Pick me up again." And so they did. Now and then they would wipe off their faces and sing:

> *Muck, mud*
> *'Tween toes*
> *Seeds swell*
> *Sprouts grow*
>
> *Take me*
> *With you*
> *With you when you go*

After a while, the muddy track became a road, which is to say that the mud was wider. Toward midday, they stopped.

"Perhaps we should go back," said Brother as they sat down to rest. Even though he was afraid of Aunt, he did not like leaving a place he knew. And he was hungry. Of course, Sister must be just as hungry. He put his rain-soaked fingers down in a pocket of the coat and pulled out the double cherry. The cherry was so shriveled and small that both parts together were still no bigger than a pea. He held it out to Sister.

"Eat," he said.

"No, you," she said.

They could not decide which one should eat it, and the cherry looked too small to split, so Brother tucked it back in the pocket. Meanwhile, Sister felt the slick, wet side of the log. Where Eldest Aunt had nicked it with the spade, Sister could feel a narrow scar.

Brother ran his fingers over a knot in the wood.

"This feels like a knee," he said.

They began to feel other odd knots in the log. One felt like an elbow, another like a heel.

The rain let up as they set out again. The water spilled off into ditches, and the road was not so muddy. Then the rain stopped, and they passed a place where pussy willows bloomed. Bits of sky turned blue, and patches of sunshine dotted the road.

They began to see flowers along the way. They passed an old plough, rusting beside a barn. A skinny cow stood in a meadow. The log began to dry out and was easier to carry.

They came to the crossroad that Uncle had said they would find. There sat a bearded man with a pack.

"Peddler!" said Sister.

"Ah, Forgottens," said the peddler. "Is it months or years? Hard to believe how much you've grown."

"Your beard is longer," said Brother. "And it's turning gray."

"I'll tell you why," the peddler answered. "This week, I haven't sold even a roofer's nail, and have eaten even less. I'm just too hungry to go on."

"Hungry?" Brother took out the cherry and gave it to the peddler. The peddler put it on his tongue, closed his eyes, and sucked. A smile spread over his face, and after a while he chewed and swallowed. Then he stood up, patted his belly, and spat two cherry pits into a puddle beside the road.

"Well, I won't starve today," he said. "Forgottens, what thanks can I give you, and why are you wandering along this road?"

"Well," Sister replied, "you can stop calling us Forgottens and call us Left-Behinds instead, for that is what we are. And we're looking for Second Uncle and Aunt."

At that instant, they heard such a dreadful scream, they all covered their ears.

"That's the saw you hear at their mill," said the peddler, pointing back where he had come from. "But if I were you, I'd go back to your eldest uncle. Your second uncle's a sour old buzzard. Ask him for bread, and he'll give you sawdust."

"Well, we can't go back," said Brother. "Eldest Aunt will peck us into sausage."

"Then I've said all I can say," said the peddler. "But once together, never apart, and better days may come."

So Brother and Sister continued on.

CHAPTER THREE

Sister & Brother
Every-Day-Missed

Sister and Brother came to a house with a shingled roof, and a shed beside it. In the yard, a round woman sat on a ladder-back chair. At her feet, a herd of babies crawled about.

"There you are, my dear," the woman called to Sister.

"There I am what?" Sister replied.

"Aren't you my new nanny?" asked the woman. "If not, then who is going to help me look after my darlings?" She pointed at the babies, drooling on the grass. "See how many!" she said. "And only I to look after them while my husband works all day in his mill."

Sister nodded and said, "It must be hard. But we're only Sister and Brother Left-Behind, and the only nanny we ever heard of was a goat. Eldest Uncle told us we should come and stay with you, if you are Second Aunt and Uncle."

"We are," said the woman. "Can you wrangle critters like these?"

Brother said, "We used to chase chickens."

He and Sister got down on all fours to chase the babies around the yard.

"And look what you've brought," the aunt said, seeing the apple log. "Husband!" she called, and said, "Boy, get up and meet your uncle. Speak as loudly as you can. He's been running that saw so many years, an ear of corn hears better than he. Husband!!" she called much louder.

A man came out of the shed, brushing sawdust off his long yellow nose. The top of his head was as bald as a buzzard.

"Husband!!!" yelled the aunt. "These are the Left-Behinds!"

The uncle frowned. "Wet behinds?" he said.

"Left-Behinds!" she repeated. And they've brought you a log."

Uncle looked around. "Where? Does it bite?"

"Not dog, log!" yelled the aunt. She pointed.

"That?" said the uncle. He looked at the log.

"Second Uncle, please," said Sister. "This log may not want to be sawed. Listen, it can talk."

"Can walk?" said the uncle. "On what?"

He picked up the apple log and was about to carry it into the shed.

"Husband!" yelled the aunt. "The girl can help me look after our sweeties! The boy can help you in the mill!" To Brother she added, "Don't worry, it's safe as a seesaw. Why, just look at my dear husband's hands. He's sawed logs into boards and such all these years, and he still has practically all of his fingers. Husband, show them your hands!"

Proudly, Uncle held up a hand. Two of the fingers were missing, and the rest looked shorter than they ought to be.

"Oh, dear," said Second Aunt, "he just lost the tip of a pinkie. Also, his left leg is made of wood." She bent down and rapped Uncle's shin. "One day, he raised it to pour the sawdust out of his cuff, and the saw just took that leg right off. But he still has one good leg to stand on."

This did not make Brother feel safe. Still, he said bravely, "Uncle, I'll help you as much as I can. But as for the log—"

"Don't mumble, boy!" said Uncle.

Evening had come. It was time for the aunt and Sister to chase the babies into the house.

"Follow me," said Second Uncle, leading Brother into the shed. But the sun was down, and the shed was too dark for working. Uncle picked up a bucket of water. He opened the hatch of a metal box beneath the sharp, round blade of the saw. Brother saw flames inside the box.

"Boy, that's the fire that makes the steam that turns this big, old saw. Pour this water in the fire box to put out the flames for the night. Then fill up the bucket again. When the rooster crows tomorrow morning, come out and light the fire again so the engine can run the saw. Then I'll come out and saw this worthless log into matchsticks."

"Not matchsticks!" said the log, but Uncle didn't hear.

"Look," said Uncle, showing Brother the top of his head. "Wonder how I got so bald? One day I bent over a little too far, and that old saw gave me a haircut. Ha! Ha! The hairs were so frightened they never grew back!"

With that, Uncle put out the fire himself, grabbed Brother by the ear, and dragged him back to the house.

⚬⚬⚬

It was not a quiet supper. The babies shrieked, spat out their bread, and threw crumbs all over the floor. They kept poor Sister so busy, she hardly got a bite herself. After supper, she and Aunt put the babies to bed, then washed the flowered table-cloth, the dishes, and a heap of diapers before Sister could go to sleep. Brother tried to get up to help Sister, but Uncle pulled him back in his chair.

"Save your muscles for the mill," said Uncle.

That night, Brother and Sister lay on the floor under Eldest Uncle's coat.

"Sister, don't fall asleep," Brother whispered. "Tomorrow, Uncle plans to cut up the apple log."

But Sister's eyes were already closed.

"Sister," pleaded Brother, "we've got to save the log."

Nothing he said could wake her. So, when Uncle and Aunt began to snore, Brother sneaked outside and into the shed. There, he felt around in the dark until he found the apple log. He dragged it outside and pushed it deep in a pile of sawdust.

In the morning when Sister awoke, Second Aunt was already up among her brood, wiping noses with one hand, stirring oat-meal with the other, and calling for Sister to help. Brother got up, went out, and built the fire in the fire box under the saw. Then Uncle came into the shed. He could see right away that the log was gone.

"You sneaked out in the night and stole it!" he said, grabbing Brother by the nose.

"No, Uncle!" Brother replied.

"Then what did you do with it?"

Brother did not know what to say. But he never liked to lie, so all he could do was say, "I buried it."

"Burned it?" cried the uncle.

"Buried it," Brother said softly again.

"You mean you chopped up the log and threw it in the fire box?" roared Uncle. "Splinter-head!"

From that day forward, Uncle scolded Brother worse each day. "Blockhead!" he would call him. "Sawdust-brain!" "Wood-wits!"

Meanwhile, day by day, Aunt treated Sister more and more kindly.

"You are as good as a second mother," Aunt would say.

"But I'm not a mother," said Sister. "And Brother has such a hard time in the mill."

"The mill is hard," the aunt agreed. "Every month, my husband cuts off some part of himself I hardly knew was there. Things were better years ago when he and I were courting."

"How were they better?" Sister asked.

"Well, back then, the farms were not so poor."

"What has made them poor?"

"Oh," said the aunt, "farms draw their life from the woods, and the woods are nothing but firewood now. In the past, there were all kinds of trees around. In spring, the trees would blossom and honey bees filled the air. How happy your uncle was back then, buzzing away with the bees! Of course, bees cannot do without blossoms, and blossoms are nothing without their bees. And, of course, none of them can do without mushrooms. In the old days, our cider mill pressed cherry juice, and honey poured out of the hives. Every summer and fall, we gathered mushrooms and ate them with honey, like bread. But all that is gone now, since the best kinds of trees were cut down and carted away."

It is hard to say how long Sister and Brother lived at the saw mill, because Uncle scolded the time off the clock. As the months passed, Sister grew fond of the babies, but then she would hear the saw in the shed, and Uncle yelling at Brother. It seemed poor Brother could do nothing right. And if Brother worked near that saw much longer, he would end up deaf as a diaper, and without any fingers, too.

One afternoon, Sister went for a walk, trying to think what to do. A new tree stood beside the road.

"What is this kind of tree?" she wondered. "It's grown so quickly, and right where the peddler spat out the cherry pits." Then she remembered the apple tree that Brother had found where the peddler had spat out the apple seeds. "This could be a cherry tree," she thought.

As she turned away, the tree rustled.

"Cut me down," it said.

"Oh, that must be the wind," thought Sister. But after that, whenever she walked nearby, the tree said the same thing again. Even in her dreams, she heard it saying, "Cut me down."

"What makes you mumble in your sleep?" Brother asked one night.

Sister replied, "It's the cherry tree, asking me to cut it down."

"Well, the moon is full," said Brother. "Sneak out and do it."

Sister waited for Aunt and Uncle to snore. Then she took Aunt's kitchen cleaver and tiptoed barefoot down the road, where the moon helped her find the tree.

"Cut me down," the cherry tree whispered.

Sister cut it down.

"Now lop me down to my trunk," it whispered.

Sister lopped off the branches, leaving nothing but the log.

"Now hide me in the field grass," said the log. "But take me with you when you go."

～❧～

Often, when Sister and Brother watched Second Aunt kissing the babies, they could not help but wonder where were parents of their own.

"Aunt," Sister asked one day, "Eldest Uncle said we were left behind. Can you tell me where or how?"

"Your parents were foolish," the aunt replied.

"What did they do?"

"Nothing. They didn't even know they had left you. It seems you just went missing."

"You mean they missed us?" asked Brother.

"That could be."

"But how can babies go missing?" asked Sister.

"That's more than I can say," said Aunt. "The one who might know is your youngest uncle, the table-maker who lives in town. But the town is too far for us to take you, and it is such a poor, gray place."

"We can go on our own," said Sister.

Second Aunt frowned. "You wouldn't leave my plumpkins, would you?" she asked. "They'd miss you so much!"

Sister did not know what to say. Every day, she worried more about Brother. Yet whenever she asked him, "Stay or leave?" he always answered, "Stay." Perhaps that was because he knew that Sister's life was not as hard as his own. Or perhaps he thought his own life could become even worse somewhere else. Besides, now they would have *two* heavy logs to carry. It seemed impossible to leave.

"At least one thing is better," said Sister to Brother one night. "At least we know we are not Left-Behinds and not Forgottens."

Brother shook some sawdust out of his ear.

"Hot frog bottoms?" he asked.

"Oh, Brother, the saw is making you deaf! What I meant to say was that someone is probably missing us every day."

"Then that is who we are," said Brother. "Brother and Sister Every-Day-Missed."

A few days later, a poor farmer stopped by with a load of hay. He led the uncle out to his cart.

"See what I found when I mowed my field," said the farmer. "I expect you'll want to buy it."

In the hay was a handsome log. Uncle took one look, pushed the farmer aside, and carried the log to the shed.

"Boy, look what I have to cut!" he said.

Sister saw him go by with the log. She ran out to the shed, crying, "Brother, that's the cherry log!"

Brother pulled at his uncle's arm. "Uncle, please don't saw that log."

"Stump-head!" the uncle replied. "Think you can burn up this one, too?"

He shook Brother loose, turned on the saw, and set up the log to cut. At the first, sharp nick of the blade, the log gave a shriek.

"Don't you hear that, Uncle?" Brother shouted.

"Boy, that was only the ring of the blade. Buzz off and let me work."

Meanwhile, the farmer was in the house with the aunt, who was making him hold all her babykins.

When the farmer heard the shriek, he ran out, shouting, "Sawyer, stop! You must pay me before you cut."

Outside the shed, the farmer rubbed his fingers together to show Second Uncle he needed some cash. Then the two of them held up fingers to show how much the farmer wanted and how much the uncle would give. Poor farmer—trying to count Uncle's fingers!

"One, two—and a knuckle—and another half-knuckle—how many is that?"

"I haven't much time!" thought Brother, alone in the shed. Then he remembered the bucket of water. He picked it up and poured it into the boiler fire. Meanwhile, Uncle finished haggling with the farmer. He came back, tried to start the saw, but nothing happened because Brother had put out the fire.

"Knot-noggin!" said Uncle. "You let the fire die out!"

Brother fell on his knees and said, "I'm sorry, Uncle. It's true that I can't do anything right."

"Well, you've worn out my patience for today," said Uncle. "I'll finish the job tomorrow. But between now and then, no tricks!"

❦

That night, Brother and Sister whispered back and forth.

"We must run away again," she said, "no matter how heavy two logs will be."

"But where?" asked Brother.

"To the table-maker, our youngest uncle. Aunt says he might know how we went missing."

"All right," he replied. "But how will we get away, with Uncle lying awake all night to keep an eye on me? See, he left a candle lit to watch me, in case I get up."

"I have an idea," she said.

A short while later, Brother got up.

"Boy, why are you up?" asked Uncle, as Brother's shadow crossed the room.

Brother opened his mouth and pointed inside it.

"Hungry?" Uncle nodded and yawned. "Then eat and buzz on back to sleep."

Brother ducked under the table and gathered two handfuls of sharp, dry crumbs that the babies had dropped on the floor. At first, he pretended to eat the crumbs. Then, behind his back, he dropped the crumbs into the cribs. No sooner had Brother lain down again than the babies woke up, itching and crying because of the crumbs.

"Girl, get up," said Second Aunt. "See if their bottoms are wet."

Sister got up and felt the babies' bottoms. "Aunt, they are dry," she said.

"Then give them bottles of milk."

Sister gave the babies bottles, but that did not quiet them, either.

"Pick up a crying baby and rock it," said Aunt. "When it falls back to sleep, put it down and rock another."

"Very well," said Sister.

She picked up a baby and rocked it. The baby went back to sleep in her arms, but when she laid it back in the crumbs, it woke up crying again. Aunt moaned, shook her husband, and rolled out of bed.

"Get up," she told him. "You, too, boy. Everyone, rock!"

They all got up to rock the babies back to sleep. But as soon as they put a baby down, it woke up crying, as before. And while it's a bad thing not to be able to sleep, it's even worse to be up all night with a mob of crying babies. Of course, Uncle hardly heard the crying. So he went back to bed, where he snored as loud as his saw. Aunt also went back to bed and covered her head with a pillow. Then, quietly, Brother and Sister picked the crumbs out of the cribs.

When all the babies were back to sleep, Brother and Sister went outside, taking Eldest Uncle's coat. They dug the apple log out of the sawdust and brought the cherry log out of the shed. As they lifted the logs to their shoulders, Aunt came out of the house with the candle and raised it to their faces.

"You're going?" she asked.

"We are," said Sister.

"I understand," said the aunt. "I shall miss you. Will you leave me Eldest Uncle's coat? It would keep my poochies warm, spread over their cribs on a chilly night. And tonight is so mild, you cannot need it. Take this instead. It's a family cloth."

It was the flowered tablecloth that she held out for them to take. Sister and Brother looked at each other and nodded.

"It's good you also take those logs," said Aunt. "They'll make good legs for Youngest Uncle's tables. Now, walk east and you will reach the town."

So Brother and Sister set off down the road. To keep themselves awake, they sang:

Stars bright
Sky glow
Stems into
Leaves grow

Take me
With you
With you when you go

Often that night, Brother wanted to stop. He felt bad about leaving a place he knew.

He said, "Who knows about aunts and uncles ahead? They might be worse than the ones we left behind."

"Still," replied Sister, "I couldn't bear to think of you losing your fingers. Let's see what lies ahead."

Later that night, they stopped and rested, wishing they had something to eat, but all they had got from the aunt was a flowered cloth. They sat on their logs in the empty road. In the starlight, Brother could just see the cut that the saw had made in the cherry log. It looked like a tear. Sister ran her fingers over the knots in the wood.

"This knot feels like the bump on my wrist," she said. "And this one goes in like a belly-button."

Brother also felt shapes in the wood.

As they set out walking again, the two logs whispered back and forth, one in a high voice, one in a low voice.

"What are they saying?" asked Brother.

"I'm not sure," Sister answered. "But I think they don't want to be tables."

The eastern sky became bright ribbons of yellow and pink. Birds sang in the bushes beside the road. The sun rose.

That afternoon, Sister and Brother climbed up a great hill and over its crest. Below them, they saw the roofs of a smoky town. Beyond the town was a harbor with steamships in the bay, and beyond the harbor was the sea. They smelled the sea salt in the air. But there were so many roofs below that they wondered how they would ever find their youngest uncle and aunt. They sat down on the hillside, to talk about what to do.

"If only the peddler were here," said Sister. "He could always tell us where to go."

"It is just as well that he isn't," said Brother. "He'd be starving and we would have nothing to give him."

But something was coming up the road, slowly. At first, it looked like a rutabaga as big as a house. Then they saw a pair of legs beneath it. It was someone wearing a pack so big that his legs looked like toothpicks underneath.

"Peddler!" Brother and Sister cried.

The old man reached them and sank to his knees. He crawled out from under his load and said, "Sister, Brother Left-Behind! Tell me, is it months or years?"

Sister replied, "Long enough that now your beard has turned more white than gray."

"I'll tell you the reason for that," he answered. "I've been peddling all my life, and still I'm as poor as ever I was. But down in that town, I spent every last penny to fill this pack with goods to sell, and I was heading out one last time. And now I can't climb another step with this load. Not on my skinny old legs. Not on this empty belly."

Brother nodded. "We, too, have nothing to eat."

"Then I must starve," said the peddler. Tears welled up in his eyes.

"But peddler," said Sister, "the crest of the hill is just behind us. Let us carry your pack to the top. You can roll it down the other side."

Without waiting for the peddler's reply, Sister and Brother got up and tried to lift the enormous pack. But the pack was so heavy, they might as well have been trying to lift the hill that they were standing on.

As the peddler watched them struggle, a change came over his face. "Brave Left-Behinds," he said. "You cannot lift my pack, and yet you lift my spirits! Now I see how things are in life. Every time we meet, you teach me not to turn back. Now I must lift this pack myself and show you that I can go on. Just help me back into the straps. Yes, and now, just push up a little on either side, and see if I don't get up!"

Slowly, with many groans and much pushing by Sister and Brother, the peddler staggered back onto his feet, under his mountain of stuff.

"What thanks can I possibly give?" he said, wobbling.

"First," said Brother, "stop calling us Left-Behinds. Call us Every-Day-Missed instead. Besides that, maybe you can help us find our youngest uncle down in that town."

"You mean your Uncle Broken-Heart."

"'Broken-Heart?'"

"Oh, yes! Go out to the end of the market street."

"What's a market street?" asked Sister.

"That's a street where shops have food in their windows that neither you nor I can eat. Near the end of that street, you'll come to a lane. There, in the window of the house at the corner, you'll see wooden tables instead of food. But if I were you, I'd go back where you came from. You'll never get even a smile from your grumpy Uncle Broken-Heart."

"But we can't go back," said Sister.

"I've said what I can," declared the peddler, shaking his head. "Now, you're bound to have more troubles than even this pack could hold. But once together, never apart, and push me toward the top!"

So Sister and Brother gave one last push and sent the peddler on his way.

CHAPTER FOUR

Uncle Broken-Heart

By the time they entered the town, Brother and Sister were mighty hungry. As they walked out the market street, they passed the shops with windows full of food, but the peddler had told them they couldn't eat there, so they passed on by with tummies growling. Near the end of the street stood a house at the corner of a lane. Its window was full of wooden tables. Each table was carved with faces.

The door was ajar, so Sister and Brother went in. Inside was a workroom—simple and bare. There, a thin man knelt in a pile of shavings, smoothing a board with a plane.

"I'm closed," he said, without looking up.

"Please, Uncle," said Sister, "We're Brother and Sister Every-Day-Missed. We've been living with Second Uncle and Aunt."

The man stopped planing but said not a word.

"And before that," added Brother, "we were Sister and Brother Left-Behind, and lived with Eldest Aunt and Uncle."

Still, the man was silent.

"And before that," Sister added, "Granny called us Brother and Sister Forgotten. We've come to you and Youngest Aunt to find out if anyone has really missed us all these years."

The man looked around and his eyes opened wide. Then he turned away and said coldly, "What Youngest Aunt? I have no wife. And suppose I were your uncle. So?"

Brother's face turned red with anger. "The peddler was right," he said. "You're grumpy from head to toe! Sister, let's go back to the sawmill."

"No," said Sister, just as angry. "I won't go back."

"Get out!" said the uncle. "Go to the orphan house—that dark old place with the iron gate at the end of the street. That's where forgotten children go."

Sister stamped her foot. "We're not forgotten!" she cried.

"Missed, forgotten, it's all the same," the uncle replied. "The orphan house is the place people go if they ever want children like you."

"Then we'd rather be there than here," said Brother. "And as for our logs, we would rather burn them up than let you turn them into table legs!"

The children turned toward the door, singing,

> *Broke heart*
> *Stubbed toe*

But their voices were choked by tears.

"Wait!" said Youngest Uncle.

The children stepped into the lane and started their song again.

> *Broke heart*
> *Stubbed toe*
> *Mean green*
> *So-and-so*

Uncle ran to the door behind them.

"What's that song you're singing?" he begged.

"Nothing! It's no song at all!"

"Nothing? Ah, right, it's nothing to me. Still, it sounds like— a tune I used to know."

"Then sing it yourself!" said Brother.

"It was so long ago," said the uncle. "I'm not sure I can. You see, my heart—my heart is too broken to sing. Please sing it for me, just once to the end."

The children looked at him angrily.

"Please?" he repeated.

"Very well," said Sister coldly. She nodded to Brother and both of them opened their mouths again.

> *Take me—*

There, they stopped and said, "Now you."

"Me?" said Uncle.

"Yes, you," said Sister. "Since you think you know it."

"Well," the uncle mumbled, "I'll try." He began to sing so timidly that his voice could barely be heard.

> *Take me*
> *With you....*

"Go on, Uncle," Brother urged.

"No, it's too hard."

"Uncle!" Sister commanded. "Now or never, you must sing!"

Uncle stared at her. At last, he said meekly, "I can't. Not anymore. But come inside. At least for the night, stay here with me, and I will look after you well."

"Why should we?" Sister replied. "In the end, you'll turn out worst of all."

Sister began to cry again, and so did Brother. Then Uncle Broken-Heart did, too.

But when Brother and Sister heard the uncle sob, they stopped crying themselves and shouted, "Stop squawking!"

Uncle stopped.

"Now, Uncle," said Sister, "you must tell us how we went missing."

Uncle Broken-Heart turned pale. "Who said I could?" he replied.

"Second Aunt," said Brother.

"Well, she's wrong. I can't."

Neither Brother nor Sister was sure what Uncle meant by 'can't.' Did he mean he didn't know how they had gone missing, or did he mean he couldn't bear to say?

Uncle wiped his eyes. "Are you hungry?" he asked.

"No!" The children turned away.

"Really? I thought I heard two bellies rumbling a moment ago."

Sister and Brother looked at each other. Of course, they had heard it, too.

"We passed so many shops with food," said Brother. "But the peddler said we couldn't eat there."

"Then come inside and eat," said the uncle.

So Brother and Sister followed him in. Upstairs in his kitchen, Uncle Broken-Heart fed them a supper of cabbage and cream. Then he showed them an empty room and laid soft pillows on the floor. It was the first night of autumn, chilly, so he gave them blankets, too. All this while, they kept the logs at their sides, in case Uncle tried to snatch them.

"Sleep well," said Uncle, stepping out of their room and closing the door behind him.

"Brother," said Sister, as they lay down, "do you think Uncle Broken-Heart means well?"

"I don't know," said Brother. "But what if we really are just Forgottens, not even Left-Behinds? And what if we were never missed—not even for one single day?"

Sister also feared this could be true. To cheer themselves up, they sang a bit of Granny's song, then said goodnight.

"Once together, never apart," they promised as they went to sleep.

❧

Next morning at breakfast, Brother and Sister asked Uncle how they could make themselves useful. When they told him all the things they had done for other uncles and aunts, he put them to work sanding wood and mixing glue. While they worked, he built frames for two new beds. Then he gave them each a carving knife and said, "Carve what you like on the bedposts."

In the evening, he sent them out to shop for supper. Before they went, he taught them enough to read whether a sign on a shop said 'Open' or 'Closed.' They had never gone shopping before. They had never even touched money. Sister liked the faces on the coins. Brother liked how a tiny coin could be traded for a head of cabbage. They also saw performers on the street— jugglers and people with puppets on strings.

"Those are called marionettes," said Uncle when they got back.

All day while he was busy, Uncle acted neither happy nor sad. But in the evening after supper, his mood became blue, and he shut himself up in his room. In their own room, Sister and Brother sat on their beds, deciding what to carve on their bedposts.

"I shall carve one of these," said Brother, looking at his own bare feet.

"First, practice on a scrap," said Sister. "That way, you won't ruin the bedpost."

"Carve me," said a voice. It came from the apple log, which Brother had hidden under his bed. Brother raised the log onto his lap.

Said Sister, "Those knots on your log could be toes."

"Carve," said the log.

So Brother began to carve, and toes began to stick out, as though the wood had a foot inside it.

"Carve me," said another voice from below. It was the cherry log, under Sister's bed. She pulled it out from under and stared at her own bare foot. Then she, too, began to carve. By midnight, the floor was covered with shavings and Brother and Sister had fallen asleep. But by that time, they had carved two pairs of wooden feet.

Next day, Uncle Broken-Heart put them back to work in his shop. In the evening, again, they went out to buy supper. All this day, too, while Uncle was busy, he had seemed neither happy nor sad. But in the evening after supper he was blue again, and again he shut himself up in his room.

Said Sister, "Tonight I shall try to carve a hand," and she raised her own hand to look at it.

"Carve me," the cherry log whispered.

Soon, Sister found knots in the log like knuckles, and she began to carve. Then Brother found the tip of a thumb on the apple log and began to carve it out as well. By midnight, when they fell asleep, they had carved two pairs of hands.

You can imagine what happened on nights after that: knees, elbows, arms, legs, ankles, bodies, and necks. Now Brother and Sister knew what they had been doing all along. They had been carving marionettes, and the only things left to carve were the heads. But heads have faces, and carving faces seemed harder than carving elbows or knees. When they looked at the two blocks of wood that were left, they could not see where to start. No cheek or chin, no nose or lip. Not a freckle could they see.

"Come in," said Uncle Broken-Heart when they knocked together at his door. He was lying in bed, as sad as every other night.

They showed him the two blocks of wood and said, "What faces can you see?"

Uncle studied the blocks.

"I see only tears," he said. "What sort of faces do you want?"

"A mother and father."

"Ah," the uncle sighed. Then he put the blocks down and said, "I can't."

"But your tables are covered with faces," said Brother.

"I can carve faces," Uncle replied, "but not the faces you want."

"So we must carve them ourselves?" asked Sister.

For a moment, it seemed that Uncle would agree, but he shook his head and murmured, "No, you cannot carve them, and neither can I."

His answer disappointed them.

Sister asked, "Do you mean that you really can't carve the faces? Or do you just not care?"

"Care?" cried Uncle Broken-Heart. "You have no idea. From the moment I saw you two in my doorway—from the moment I saw you again—" But he could not go on.

"What do you mean by 'again'?" Brother asked.

"Please, Uncle," begged Sister, "who are we?"

Uncle was silent a long time. Then he said, "The truth is simply that both of you have always been terribly missed. And you were right to ask me to carve these faces. Perhaps I can do it if I dare."

"Then will you?" they asked.

Uncle drew a long, deep breath and answered, "I will try."

CHAPTER FIVE

Youngest Uncle's Tale

That night, Sister and Brother left the blocks of wood with Uncle. They were sure that he could carve the heads. But in the morning, he came out and said nothing. He hadn't slept all night, and his face was as gray as a smudge. All day, he was tired and slow. That evening, he picked at his supper, then closed himself back in his room. Later that evening, Brother and Sister knocked at his door again.

"Come in," he said.

He was lying in bed with the blocks of wood.

"Uncle Broken-Heart," said Sister, "please tell us what is wrong."

"Wrong?" he replied. "I don't know where to begin!"

Brother and Sister climbed up on either side of Uncle and waited for him to speak.

"You see," the uncle said at last, "I was born on a mountain, out at the wild end of the world. Our parents raised four of us children there, and we each grew up and went away. My eldest brother was first to leave. He went down to the forest and married a girl with a voice like a songbird, whose family gathered apples and truffles. But the apple trees were cut down for their wood, and then the truffles disappeared. At last, all eldest brother could do was cut down firewood for a living. As for his wife, she always wanted children, but new life wouldn't grow in these woods. So she never had any, and lost her beautiful voice as well."

"Yes," said Sister. "Now she only caws."

"Go on," said Brother, patting Youngest Uncle's hand.

"Then came my second-eldest brother," Uncle went on. "Second brother grew up and walked down to the farms and married a girl whose family gathered honey, and pressed wild cherries into cider. And he fell in love with the buzz of the bees. But the cider mill got changed into a sawmill and the cherry trees were taken for lumber. Without cherry blossoms, the bees disappeared and took their honey with them. Then the sawmill ran out of wood, and the only thing left was a houseful of babies."

"We know," said Brother. "Now Second Uncle does nothing all day but perch by that terrible saw."

"Go on," said Sister, patting Broken-Heart's hand. "You must have been the third-eldest son."

"I was," he replied.

"But you said four sons in all," said Brother.

"Not four sons. Four children. The youngest was a sister and my dearest friend. We grew up happy in the wild, once together and never apart. One day she wanted to travel and see the world. I said to her, 'Let's go together.' So we came to this town by the sea, and I took up this work making tables."

"Then where is she now, and what did she want to do?" asked Brother.

"Where she is, I do not know. As for what she did, at first she couldn't decide, although she found work as a maid. After that, she became a singer."

"What did she sing?" asked Sister.

"She sang the song you sang to me. I carved a pair of marionettes to twirl about while she sang. But one day after that, she—No, I can't bear to say more."

"Go on, Uncle," they said.

"No."

"Say!"

"She...."

"She what?"

Uncle took a deep breath. "She fell in love."

"'Fell in love?' What's that?"

"I hardly know," said Uncle, "for I hated the man she loved."

"Was he mean to you?" asked Brother.

"No."

"Was he mean to her?" asked Sister.

"No. He was simply a household gardener where Sister worked as a maid. From then on, she sang for the gardener—not for me and my marionettes."

Sister sat up straight and said, "Take us to the house where they work."

"Oh, they're not there now. They didn't want to spend their entire lives as servants. They had dreams. My sister could sing like a spirit, and her gardener could dance like a prince. So she sang and he danced in the street for coins. But that didn't earn much money. And in town, one needs money to live."

"So what did they do?"

"Well, the gardener had an idea. He'd heard of a place across the sea where the people loved nothing better than pigs that could dance."

"Pigs?"

"Yes, folks would pay plenty to watch a couple of fine waltzing hogs. So the gardener decided they would go there. They would take along piglets and teach them to dance."

"Could he really teach pigs to dance?" asked Brother.

"My boy," said Broken-Heart, "he could teach turtles to tango. So they married and saved their money in order to travel there by steamship. But by that time, you had been born."

"Us?"

"You mean—" said Sister.

"Meanwhile," Uncle went on quickly, "I kept about my business, hoping they would change their minds and grow apart so Sister might come back to me. But once you were born—"

"Us!" said Brother and Sister.

"You. You smashed my hopes just like squashing a bug. So I did the only thing I could. I decided to make my sister every bit as sad as I was. The evening the ship was set to depart, I helped them carry their things on board. Your mother carried you, wrapped in blankets together, asleep. Your father carried a pair of piglets in a sack. I carried the baggage."

"Let's go find the ship!" said Sister, bouncing on the bed.

"Wait," said Uncle. "The ship was about to sail. Her horn was blowing. Her flags were flying. Black smoke poured out of her stacks as her great steam engines rumbled below. Her name was *The Wild Hope*."

"*The Wild Hope!*"

"Yes. And just before *The Wild Hope* sailed, I said to my sister, 'Sister, give me the pigs. My heart will break unless I have them to remember you by.' Poor Sister, she couldn't stand to see me cry. She gave me the sack with the sleeping piglets. We said good-bye and I hurried ashore."

"You took the piglets?" said Brother. "Then who would the gardener teach to dance?"

"It's worse than that," said Uncle. "A moment before, while your mother and father were answering the captain's questions, I had secretly switched you sleeping babies with the sleeping pigs. I wrapped the piglets in your blankets and put you in their sack."

"You stole us?" Sister and Brother cried. They jumped off the bed.

"I did," said Uncle. "Fast as I could, I ran off the ship, and the crew raised the gangway behind me. Whistles blew. The ropes were cast off from the dock, and *The Wild Hope* headed out to sea. And I ran home."

"You're mean, Uncle Broken-Heart!" said Sister.

Youngest Uncle hung his head.

"How soon did they know we were gone?" asked Brother.

"Not soon enough. Not until the pigs woke up on the ship and squealed."

"Then didn't the ship turn around?" Sister asked.

"Dear girl, big steamships never turn back. It steamed to an island many weeks east before your parents could get off. From there, they wrote back to me, saying they would return as soon as they earned enough money to travel home. But I never heard from them again. To this day, I don't know where they are."

"Did you go looking?" asked Sister.

"No. I was too much ashamed."

"Because you stole us!" said Brother.

"Yes. And because I was jealous and sad from being left behind."

"That's a very bad reason!" Sister scolded. "Very bad!"

"Well, I raised you as long as I could," said Uncle.

"I'll bet that wasn't long," she replied. "Unless you're very fond of diapers!"

"You're right," he said. "Too many diapers for me. At least be glad I didn't abandon you at the orphan house. No, I took you to Granny's and left you there for her to love. But I've been sorry ever since I took you off the ship, and sorrier after I gave you up."

There was love in Broken-Heart's words, but Brother and Sister turned away.

"We'll find them," Sister vowed.

"But what do they look like?" asked Brother.

"Well," said Uncle. "I'm not much with words. Of course, one was a woman and one was a man. They both had hands and feet and heads and so forth. Apart from that, it's hard for me to say."

Brother and Sister could not let go of their anger.

"Wicked Uncle!" Sister cried.

"Bad Uncle!" said Brother. "You deserve your broken heart."

They ran back to their room and slammed the door behind them.

A short while later, Uncle knocked.

"Please, let me in," he begged.

"No!"

"Please."

"Uncle, go away!"

So Uncle Broken-Heart returned to his own room. Brother threw himself into bed and burrowed under the covers. Sister sat in her bed and stared at her pieces of marionette. But after a while, she sat on the edge of Brother's bed and patted him where he lay.

She said, "I think that Uncle must have been very close to his sister—as close as you and I. So I think we must forgive him."

"I know," mumbled Brother. "But what after that?"

Porcabella & Mudworth

Making breakfast for someone is a good way to let him know you might forgive. So early next morning, Brother and Sister got busy in the kitchen. But when they called their uncle to eat, he did not come out of his room.

"Uncle, are you up?" Sister asked at his door.

No answer.

"Uncle?" Brother knocked.

They opened the door for a peek, but Youngest Uncle wasn't there.

"He must have gone out early," said Sister. "He's sure to come back."

They ate their breakfasts and went downstairs. On Uncle's workbench were two carved and painted wooden heads. One was the head of a man with a round face, dark curly hair, and dark mustache.

"He did it!" said Sister. "See, this was the apple block." She pointed to a pale scar that ran out from the side of one eye.

"That's the mark that Eldest Aunt made when she struck the apple log with the spade."

The other head was of a woman—a longer face with large, sad eyes.

"And this one came from the cherry block," said Brother. He knew that because on one cheek was a tear-shaped scar. It was the nick from Second Uncle's saw.

Brother and Sister ran upstairs and brought down all the other puppet parts. All day, they drilled small holes and tied the parts together with string.

"They'll catch a chill," said Brother, once the puppets were assembled. "What shall we give them for clothes?"

Then Sister remembered the flowered cloth that Second Aunt had given to them in place of Eldest Uncle's coat.

"Aunt said it was a tablecloth," she said. "Still, who knows? Our mother and father might have worn clothes of the very same kind. Didn't Granny's old, faded skirt have flowers?"

So they cut squares out of the tablecloth and made clothes for the marionettes. Then they tied long strings to the ends of some sticks that they found in Uncle's box of scrap. They tied the other ends of the strings to the arms and legs of the marionettes. That way, they could make the puppets stand and move.

That evening, Sister pulled on a string. The long-faced woman raised one hand as though she wanted to sing. Brother pulled on a string. The curly-haired man raised a knee as though he wanted to dance.

"Make the woman talk," said Brother.

Sister made the woman wave and say, "Hello."

Brother made the man bow and say, "Will anyone join me in dancing a polka?"

"We need to give them names," said Sister.

This was hard. At first, all the names they could remember were names like Feather-brains and Wood-wits.

"Those don't sound right," said Brother. "After all the troubles they've been through as logs—and all that rain and mud—I'm sure they're worth better names than that."

"Mudworth!" said Sister. "That's his name." She made the woman twirl around and sing, "Mudworth, Mudworth, Mudworth!"

"Mudworth!" Brother made the man say. "Yes, of course, that's me. So you, my dear, are Porcabella!" Brother made his Mudworth puppet dance around the woman.

"Yes, that's me," said Sister, speaking for Porcabella.

By now, the marionettes seemed almost to speak for themselves.

Mudworth stopped and bowed. "Dear Porcabella, will you sing while I dance?"

"Gladly," said Porcabella. Then she looked up at the children and said, "But who are these giants?"

"Oh, them," said Mudworth. "Don't mind about them. They're just two children, a brother and sister." He scratched his head. "But where did they come from? I wonder."

Porcabella shrugged and sighed. "I don't know," she said. "But suddenly I feel as though I've forgotten something strange and important."

"That's funny," said Mudworth, "I can't remember a thing about what we have been, or thought, or done before now."

"I can tell you why," said Sister. "We and Uncle Broken-Heart carved you. Your only past was your lives as seeds and trees."

"Trees?" replied Mudworth.

"Tell us," said Porcabella, "who is this Uncle Broken-Heart?"

So the children told them all about their uncle, what he had done, and how he had disappeared.

"Sad," said the marionettes.

"Yes," Sister agreed. "And we can't even say what our mother and father looked like."

"Ah," said Mudworth. "It doesn't seem right you should be without parents. Shall we help out for a while?"

"You could try," said Brother.

Porcabella turned her head. "Parents? That sounds very hard."

"Don't worry," said Sister. "You won't need to think much about it, since we will be pulling your strings."

"Very well," said Mudworth. "But there must be things we need to know. Please give us a rule or two."

"We don't really follow rules," said Sister. "Wait, there's one. It's 'Once together and never apart.'"

"I've thought of another," said Brother. "'Take me with you when you go.'"

"Once together, never apart," the puppets repeated. "Take me with you when you go."

"Oh, I like that," sighed Porcabella. "I like the mystery."

"Yes," said Mudworth raising his head to yawn. "It's quite a lot to think about."

Porcabella caught Mudworth's yawn. She yawned herself and

dipped her head. They were worn out by so much happening to them at once, and so much thinking for two wooden heads.

"Time for bed," said Brother.

They laid out Mudworth and Porcabella in Uncle Broken-Heart's bed. Then they cooked up some cabbage and cream and sat at the table for supper. They left some for Youngest Uncle, too, in case he came home that night. But midnight came, and Uncle did not return. Finally, the children went to bed. In case Uncle came back home later that night, they left the marionettes in his bed to keep it warm.

In the morning, Uncle Broken Heart still had not returned. Brother was just about to wake up Mudworth, when Sister had a thought.

"Brother, before we get them up, let's go to the orphan house. Remember how Uncle said he might have left us there when we were babies? It must be a place where parents look when their children go missing. Maybe our parents came back once and looked for us there. If they did, then someone there can tell us what they looked like."

"Good idea," said Brother.

They went out and around to the end of the street. There was the tall, dark house they had seen when they first came to town. They walked to the tall iron fence around it and rang a bell beside the gate. A girl came out of the house. She looked about the same age as they, or maybe a little younger.

"Can I help you?" she asked through the fence.

"What are those?" asked Sister, seeing ropes that hung down behind the girl's ears.

"These? These are my braids."

Brother's eyes lit up. He had never seen braids before, and he couldn't take his gaze away.

"Are they part of your hair?" he asked.

"Of course. See?" She held out an end of a braid through the fence.

Suddenly, Sister felt that she, too, ought to have braids. She wondered how they were made. At the same time, she was feeling annoyed with Brother and the girl, though she could not say exactly why. But instead of speaking her mind, she said, "Silly old braids!"

"Have our parents come here looking for us?" Brother asked.

"How would I know who they are?" said the girl.

"Well," he answered, "they might have been carrying pigs."

"Parents do come looking," the girl replied. "But none has come with pigs. As for me, I'm the only orphan left here now. I'm all alone this morning because the orphan house woman went out to buy eggs, and I stayed behind for the cat. It loves to play with my braids. Can you wait until the woman returns and unlocks the gate?"

"No," said Sister. The more the girl spoke, the more Sister wanted to be off with Brother, looking for parents somewhere else.

"I'm sure you'd like it here," said the girl. "Have you had breakfast?"

"Breakfast!" Brother licked his lips.

"I mean pancakes, " said the girl.

Sister didn't like how widely Brother smiled when the orphan girl talked about pancakes.

"The orphan house woman braids my hair," said the girl. "Look, here she comes."

A woman was coming up the street—tall and pretty, with a basket balanced on top of her head. Sister pulled Brother away.

"It's time to leave," she said.

"Why?" said Brother.

"Shame on you, Brother. Don't you remember? We do have parents after all, and it's time we got them out of bed. They promised to take us down to the dock. Such lazybones! Without us, they would lie in bed all day."

The braided girl frowned, for she could tell that Sister was jealous. As for Brother, he had never seen Sister jealous, so he had no idea why she was acting like this. He followed her away, whispering, "Sister, what's wrong?"

"Feather-brain!" she replied. "Our parents went off on a ship. Maybe Uncle plans to do the same. We ought to go down to the dock and see what we can learn."

"Very well," agreed Brother. "But promise we'll come back."

Sister frowned. "Why should we? That silly girl knows nothing."

Back at Uncle's house, they woke up the marionettes.

"High time you're back!" said Mudworth. "Where have you been?"

Before they could answer, Porcabella added, "We were worried sick about you. Really, you mustn't run off like that. We must watch your every move!"

"But you were asleep," said Sister.

"Then you should have waked us up," said Mudworth. "You must keep us informed."

"You're not quite our parents," said Brother.

"Maybe not," said Sister. "But we shouldn't mind if they want to practice."

"Please?" said Porcabella. "We'll do whatever you want!"

"Very well," said Sister. "Wait here at home, while we go to the dock."

"The dock?" said Mudworth. "A dangerous place! We must lead you there and back, in order to keep you out of trouble. Then we'll stop at the orphan house, to make sure you get something to eat."

Sister looked at Brother. She was angry at what he had made Mudworth say, so she made Porcabella reply, "Eat later? No! Let's have a good lunch before we go. Then the children won't whine and be hungry later, and we'll have no need of orphan people."

Then Sister spoke in her own voice, replying, "Very well, Mother. After lunch, you and Father will lead us down to the dock."

CHAPTER
SEVEN

The Wild Hope

That afternoon, Brother and Sister let Mudworth and
Porcabella lead them down to the dock. It was hard to walk like
that, holding the marionettes out front. The children could not
help kicking their parents' wooden heels.

"Walk farther behind us," the puppets complained.

"But how can we walk any farther behind?"

"Don't argue. Do as we say. Also, call us Mother and Father,
and be careful not to swing us about. You are making us dizzy."

It was not the children's fault that Porcabella and Mudworth
were swinging. It was the work of the autumn wind. Near the
dock, they passed under a tree with falling yellow leaves.

"This seems familiar," said Mudworth.

"It should," said Sister, "since you and Mother used to be trees."

Porcabella sighed. "I wonder, how would we feel to be
trees again?"

The afternoon was sunny and cool, with bright clouds over-
head. There were two large steamships at the dock. One was

tied up at the near end. Its gangway was down, and a line of passengers waited with tickets and baggage to carry aboard. The other steamship was tied up out at the distant end of the dock. The children approached the nearest ship to see if Uncle might be in line.

"Children, don't run on the dock," said Porcabella. "You'll trip and skin your knees."

A passenger smiled, watching the puppet woman scold the boy and girl. Brother and Sister searched the line, but Uncle wasn't in it.

"Let's ask the name of the ship," said Sister.

"Ahem," said Mudworth. "We have a few rules ourselves. And one is, never talk to strangers."

"But we must find out the name of the ship. She could be *The Wild Hope*."

"You must also obey your parents," he replied, and folded his arms.

"Very well," said Sister. "Mother, please go to those people for us and ask the name of the ship."

"Of course, my dear," said Porcabella.

Sister turned and walked Porcabella closer to the line. Then Porcabella began to sing:

> *Sea rise*
> *Tide flow*
> *We to an*
> *Island go*

The passengers had been bored with waiting until the puppets arrived. Now, they laughed and clapped.

"Dear travelers," said Porcabella, "What is the name of this ship?"

A man bowed and said, "Madam, this ship is called *The Royal Adventure*." He grinned and tossed a penny to Sister.

Sister took the coin back to Brother.

"Look," she said. "With a few more of these, even we might get on a ship. Go ask them again if this ship is *The Wild Hope*."

"But you already asked," said Brother.

"Never mind. You'll be funny if you ask again, because it will make you look silly. Or does Father let you speak only to little girls with braids?"

Brother's face turned red.

"No," he said, and to show that he was as brave as Sister, he danced Mudworth up to the line and made him whistle and skip.

More passengers laughed.

"Good people," said Mudworth, "what is the name of this ship?"

"Little man," said a lady, "your wife has already asked." Then she laughed and tossed a penny to Brother. "Boy, girl," she said, "make the little man and woman argue."

Brother stepped back to Sister, saying, "Bring Porcabella back."

But Sister was thinking of braids she didn't have. She handed Porcabella to Brother and said, "Here, you do them both!" Then she turned and marched away.

"Sister!" Brother called out.

What could he do with two marionettes when it took both hands to work just one? But sister would not come back. Meanwhile, another boy had been watching Sister and Brother. He was about their age or a little older. He was a corn boy, selling snacks of toasted corn to people waiting on the dock. His clothes were tattered and patched.

"Hello," he said, stepping up to Sister and handing her a bag of corn.

"Hello," she said.

"What about him?" the corn boy asked, pointing at Brother. "Would he like a bag?"

"Oh, he's never hungry," she said. "Let's race to the end of the dock!"

With that, they raced away. By the ship at the other end of the dock, they stopped to catch their breath.

"I shall be a sailor one day," said the corn boy, pointing out to sea. "That's the best life for a homeless boy like me."

"Then so shall I," said Sister.

"What ship will you sail on?" he asked.

"*The Wild Hope* – if she ever returns."

"'Ever returns?'" He laughed.

"Why are you laughing at me?" she said.

"Silly! Look!" He pointed at some tall, gold letters above them on the bow of the ship. "That's she—*The Wild Hope*. She's been in port for a week, and any moment she'll be gone."

"Are you sure?"

"Of course! Can't you read? Have you never been to school?"

"What's school?" asked Sister.

The corn boy laughed harder. At that moment, the last few passengers were climbing the gangway of *The Wild Hope*.

"Brother!" Sister yelled. "It's *The Wild Hope!*"

Sister threw away her corn and ran toward the gangway. Above her, sailors leaned out from the ship to draw up the gangway so the ship could depart.

"Wait!" she cried, and, "Brother, run!"

The sailors laughed. "Wait? The captain has given the order to sail! Your parents should have kept you on board and not let you wander the dock. Jump lively, off we go!"

"But my brother's coming!"

By this time, Brother was galloping down the dock. Mudworth and Porcabella flew like kites behind him.

"Slow down!" they cried. "You're making us dizzy again!"

"Faster, Brother!" Sister yelled.

Then Mudworth got snagged on a loading cart and was torn from Brother's grip. Porcabella got snagged on a crate, and she, too, flew out of his hand. But Brother had no time to stop. He reached *The Wild Hope* and leapt up onto the rising end of the gangway. The ship rumbled and sidled away from the dock. It headed out to sea with smoke pouring out of its stacks.

"Mudworth! Porcabella!" Sister and Brother shouted.

The marionettes shrank small behind them. Soon, Brother and Sister could barely see the dock. An hour more, the town disappeared from view, beyond the ocean's rim.

The Man in Cabin 5

"What now?" Brother scolded. "Once together, never apart! That's how we promised to stay together. You're lucky you didn't get carried out to sea without me. And Porcabella and Mudworth are gone."

"It was you who left them behind," said Sister.

"But you who rushed us down to the dock," he answered. "And then you ran off with that corn boy."

"I did not," said Sister. "I was just being nice to someone who was nice to me."

"And I, too, with the orphan girl," he replied.

Then both their faces turned pink because, for the first time, they had made each other unhappy. And that made each of them think of how Youngest Uncle and his sister, their very own mother, also had made each other unhappy.

They glanced at each other and slowly moved closer together.

"Sister," said Brother, "it's hard for me to imagine, but even Second Uncle once went off and fell in love and got married, and left his own brother and sister behind."

Sister nodded. "And it's hard for me to imagine, but one day, years and years ago, our Eldest Aunt had a heart that fell in love with Eldest Uncle, and moved away from sisters or brothers of her own."

"So it might happen to us," said Brother.

"And I hope you won't act like Youngest Uncle if I am the one to fall in love," said Sister.

"No!" said he. "I'll be glad that you are happy. And if it happens first to me," he added, "will you be happy for me?"

"I think so," she replied. "For whatever happens in the future, you will be my only brother."

"And you my only sister."

"Once together and never apart."

Brother and Sister joined hands and turned to look out to sea.

Around them, families of poor people sat on bundles on the deck, watching the sun go down behind *The Wild Hope*. Children tugged on their parents' sleeves and saying, "Mama, Papa, look."

"Mama.... Papa...." Brother and Sister whispered. It was the first time they had heard those words for parents.

A supper line was forming. Sailors were passing out bread and bowls of soup. All the families were joining the line, so Brother and Sister joined it, too.

When they got to the pot, a sailor said, "Where are your grown-ups? You can't get served without them."

"We forgot," said Sister.

"Well, show me your tickets," said the sailor.

"We forgot them, too," said Brother.

"Then step out of line."

A moment later, a deep voice said behind them, "No parents?"

It was a man in white pants and a dark blue jacket with bright brass buttons. He also had on a bright, white cap with a shiny, black brim. He stood with his hands behind his back, waiting for them to speak.

"Our parents *were* on board," said Brother finally, not far from the truth.

"Not good enough," said the man. "You see, I'm the captain, I cannot let you be on board without parents, unless you have tickets of your own."

The children shook their heads.

"Or money to buy them?"

They each held out the penny they had earned at the dock.

The captain wagged his finger. "Not enough. Your fare would cost many of those!"

"Then take us back," said Brother.

The captain frowned. "Back? Even if you two were grown-ups, even I could not turn *The Wild Hope* around." He wrinkled his brows and stroked his short, black beard. "But I won't let you starve. Follow me."

He led them down an iron ladder into the ship. There was a narrow kitchen, which sailors call a galley. The captain said a few words to a man in an apron and tall white hat. Then the captain went back up on deck.

"So, the captain says you're stowaways," said the man. "See this apron and this white mushroom hat? They make me the cook. And the captain says I should feed you, if you say 'please'."

"Please," they said.

So they were fed.

After they had eaten, the cook put Brother in front of a heaping tub of dishes. Some were made of glass, and some were made of silver, and every one of them was dirty. All these dishes were used in the dining room where the rich class of passengers ate. He put Sister in front of another heaping tub, full of dirty dishes made from wood and tin. They were for the poorer travelers who had to eat on deck.

"Get busy," said the cook.

Brother and Sister looked around and saw dozens of other tubs of dirty dishes to wash.

"Isn't there something more fun we can do?" asked Sister.

Said the cook, "There's a *worse* job, down in the bilge."

"What's the bilge?" asked Brother.

"Boy, the bilge is the deepest bottom of the ship. Down there is where the seawater goes, whenever it happens to wash on board. Down there in the bilge is also where the oil and slime collect. There are other stowaways down there right now, working the bilge pump night and day. Night and day, they pump out water and slime to keep the ship from sinking. If you'd rather do that, go down and trade places," said the cook.

All evening, Brother and Sister washed until all the dishes were finally clean.

"Good job," said the cook. "Now find yourselves a place to sleep and come back down here to the galley at dawn."

On the highest deck of the ship, the children remembered seeing cabins, with rich-looking passengers strolling about.

"Which cabin is ours?" asked Sister.

"Cabin?" The cook laughed grimly. "Follow me."

He led them down another stairway, deeper into the ship. They entered a long, low room with an iron ceiling and iron floor, and rows of iron bunks.

"This is where poor folk sleep," said the cook.

Most of the bunks were already full. Brother and Sister found an empty spot, lay down, and tried to asleep. But the lamps were on all night, and the bunks were hard, and down below, the bilge pump thumped and thumped. They missed the cozy beds that Uncle Broken-Heart had made them.

From then on, every day was work and work and more work. But the cook didn't let them starve. He grew very fond of them and treated them as well as he could. Each afternoon, he sent them up on the open deck for a breath of air and a look at the sea. Other people were up there, too, counting whales and flying fish. But seeing all the families around them on deck made Brother and Sister lonely. They wished more than ever that they could have a family of their own.

By now, it was nearly end of autumn. The ocean air was foggy and cold, and icebergs floated by. Brother and Sister wished they still had Eldest Uncle's coat, Granny's old shawl, or even the rest of the tablecloth that they had cut up to make clothes for the marionettes.

One afternoon on deck, Sister looked out at the empty sea and said, "Brother, I dreamed I heard Mama singing last night. Then I woke up, and I could still hear her, under the sea. What do you think that means?"

"It means you heard the whales," said Brother. "Cook said we might hear them singing last night."

Sister nodded. "Then he must be right. And what ever made us think we could find our own Mama or Papa, since we don't even know what they look like?" Then she thought about the marionettes and how much she had loved their faces.

"I know what else you're thinking," said Brother. "We should have taken better care of Mudworth and Porcabella. We lost them, just as our parents lost us once. Do you think they're still caught on the dock? Or have they been blown away by a storm or picked apart by seagulls?" To fight back a tear, he began to sing, and Sister joined his song.

> *Wave high*
> *Wave low*
> *Wind, where*
> *Ever blow*
>
> *Take me*
> *With you*
> *With you when you go*

They sang it over and over, loud enough to hear above the rumbling engines, the wind, and the dashing of waves at the bow. Other passengers strolled by and stopped to listen, but

Brother and Sister kept on singing until the captain called down from the pilot house.

"You sound a bit lonely," he called.

They looked up and nodded.

"You see," replied Brother, "our parents sailed away one day, and we were left behind."

"But we've always been missed," added Sister. "At least we think so. We're hoping to find them as soon as we land."

"Land?" said the captain. "No land for you. You must stay on board washing dishes for as long as it takes to pay for the voyage."

"How many more dishes is that?" Brother asked.

"Plenty more."

"How long will it take?"

"Twelve years."

"Twelve years?" cried Sister.

"Don't blame me. I'm only the captain, and those are the rules on *The Wild Hope*."

"Twelve years?" repeated Brother as the captain turned away.

Sister and Brother headed back across the deck. What made things harder was that, all around them, everyone else was happy. *The Wild Hope* had entered the tropics, where the weather is always warm. At midnight, there would be a party on board as *The Wild Hope* crossed the equator. All around, childrend were begging their parents to let them stay up late.

In the galley, Brother asked, "Cook, is there any way to wash twelve years of dishes in less than twelve years?"

The cook shook his head and said, "There's not, but I know how you feel. I've been stuck in this galley forever. Somehow, I

just can't seem to get off this ship. But never mind. The party
will cheer you up."

It was almost midnight by the time the supper dishes
were clean.

"Here's an idea," said the cook. "Would you like to earn some
extra money?" He held out a dish of old brown fruit that he had
chopped into bits. "The man in cabin 5 has been ill ever since
we left port. He stays in his cabin, and all he can eat are these
old, dry pieces of fruit. Take this dish to him for a snack, and
maybe he'll give you a tip." He handed the dish to Sister, saying,
"Hurry, he's always in bed by midnight. And remember, cabin 5."

"What's a 5?" she asked.

"What's a 5?" The cook was amazed. "So grown, and you
don't know your numbers? Watch this." He picked up a tube of
icing and squirted a 5 on the back of a plate. "Now lick it off,"
he said. "That way, you'll remember the shape."

Sister and Brother licked off the 5, and went up to the main
deck with the dish. There, a band was playing. Crowds were
already dancing or watching the ocean over the sides of the
ship. They held lanterns over the water, hoping to see a long
orange line, for that's what they thought the equator must be.

"What shall we sing?" a man asked. "Captain," he called up to
the pilot house, "isn't there a special song to sing when we cross
the line?"

"No," the captain called down.

"There should be!" people cried.

Then a young girl noticed Brother and Sister, on their way

up the stairs past the captain's lookout, and on up from there to the cabins.

"Remember those two?" cried the girl. "They were singing this afternoon—a song about a journey!"

"You two!" said the captain, stopping Brother and Sister as they passed the pilot house door. "Sing it again!"

Sister and Brother were speechless. They felt much too sad to sing. And if they didn't reach cabin 5 by midnight, the sick old man would be asleep by the time they knocked. Then he'd be angry that they had waked him up, and there would be no tip.

"Sing!" shouted the crowd on the deck below.

Brother and Sister looked at each other.

"Well?" said Sister.

"Well," said Brother, "Granny always told us to sing when we're lonely or sorry or lost."

So they opened their mouths and sang.

> *Earth turn*
> *Breeze blow*
> *Brave seeds*
> *Wind sow*
>
> *Take me*
> *With you*
> *With you when you go*

The crowd caught onto the chorus and sang:

> *Take me*
> *With you*
> *With you when you go*

Then someone shouted, "There's the equator!" and everyone ran to the railings to look. Everyone except Brother and Sister. As fast as they could, they climbed to cabin 5 and pounded on the door.

"Go away," said a voice. "I'm asleep."

Sister and Brother stared at the door. Then they turned and headed back down with the dish to the dancing and singing below.

"Join the fun!" said a gentleman, grabbing Sister's arm.

The dish went flying, scattering bits of fruit across the deck. Brother and Sister sank down on all fours and scrambled to pick up the bits beneath the dancers' feet.

"Well, perhaps twelve years won't seem long," said Sister as she wedged her way among the dancers. "But by the time we find our parents, we'll both be looking and acting like grown-ups ourselves."

"True," Brother agreed. "Let's hope we can act like nice ones!"

By now, they were both about ready to crawl back down to their iron bunk and sadly sing themselves to sleep.

Suddenly, a voice rang out.

"Who taught you that song?" a woman was asking the crowd.

"Just now?" someone answered. "You mean, 'Take me with you when you go'?"

"The very song we mean," said a man.

Then the captain called down from above, "Get back to the bilge, you two!"

"No!" cried the woman. "We've been pumping down there for so long, we ache so much, it's as though our joints were made of wood!"

"But you must finish your time," said the captain.

"Dear, the captain's right," said the man. "We must go back down to the bilge. The sooner we serve out our years down there, the sooner we may find our children."

"I won't go down!" the woman replied. "Not until these people have told us where they learned our song."

"From our dishwashers," the captain replied.

"A boy and a girl?"

"No more questions!" the captain commanded. "Come up here straight away. I must teach you to obey my orders!"

Brother and Sister stood up. Now they could see the man and woman climbing the stairs to the captain. *Clomp-clomp* went their big, black, rubber boots. Sister and Brother could hardly believe their eyes. Apart from those boots—and the fact that this man and this woman were people and had no strings—they looked exactly like Porcabella and Mudworth!

"Porcabella! Mudworth!" Sister and Brother shouted.

The crowd stood back. The captain looked down.

"Who?" he thundered.

The man looked down. "Mudworth?" he said. "My name isn't Mudworth."

"And mine isn't Porcabella," added the woman. "But you— you two...." She stared down at the children.

"Sister, don't you see?" said Brother. "The faces Uncle Broken-Heart carved, Mudworth and Porcabella's—he was trying to tell us what Mama and Papa looked like!"

"Mama? Papa?" Sister cried.

They ran across the deck and up the captain's stairs.

"My babies!" the woman cried. "Who else could have known our song?"

"Babies?" cried the man, as Brother and Sister reached the pilot house. "My boy! My girl!"

Brother and Sister jumped into their parent's arms.

"Mama, Mama," Sister cried, "see how a tear rolls down your cheek and fits in that little scar."

"And you, Papa," said Brother, "all these years, every night when you lay down, your tears have worn a groove just like the scar by Mudworth's eye."

"Mudworth?" said Papa. "Who is this Mudworth?"

Brother began to explain, when suddenly, above them all, the door to cabin 5 flew open, and out came a man in a bathrobe— barefoot, with a snowy white beard.

"Ahoy!" he cried. "What are all this noise and to-do that are keeping a sick old man awake?"

Brother and Sister stared up at the man.

"Peddler!"

The peddler stared down. "Brother and Sister Every-Day-Missed? Is it you?"

"It is!" they shouted. "And look who we found!"

The peddler laughed. "Captain," he said, "please send your noisy crowd to bed!"

The captain looked up and tipped his hat, as captains do for the rich. Then he looked down on the crowd and said, "We've crossed the equator. The party's over. Everyone, good night!"

CHAPTER NINE

The Peddler's Tale

A short while later, the family and the captain gathered in the peddler's cabin. The parents sat on the bed with Sister and Brother in their laps. The cook stood listening at the door.

"I know you," Mama told the peddler. "You used to come around our home on the mountain, when I and my brothers were growing up. But how do you know my children?"

"Madam," the peddler replied, "think of me as a sort of grampa to Brother and Sister Found. You see, whenever they were lost, I was there to show them the way."

"And to eat," Brother added.

"But how did you get on this ship?" Papa asked.

"How?" said the peddler. "It's a mystery to me as well. How could a poor old man, like me, have carried that huge pack one more step up that hill? A donkey couldn't have done it! Then there they were, this boy and girl, getting me back on my feet. 'Well!' I said to myself. 'With friends like these, how can I let myself give up?' So I made it to the top of that hill, and the pack and I rolled down the other side to the farms in the valley below. And what do you know? Down there, new life had spread out in all directions. Everywhere, bees, trees, mushrooms, pigs, people, and everything else were growing back and doing well. In a matter of days, I'd sold off everything I had."

"So you got rich?" asked Sister.

"As rich as a king's little toe. But when I came to your second aunt and uncle's sawmill, I found out something amazing. Remember your sweet second aunt?"

Brother and Sister nodded.

Said the peddler, "She told me the strangest story. One day, a cherry tree suddenly grew near the mill. Next morning, the cherry tree was gone, but right after that, another cherry tree stood in its place, bursting with fat, red cherries."

"Strange," said Papa. "I wonder, who or what planted those magic trees?"

The peddler, Brother, and Sister just smiled.

Then the peddler shook his head and added, "Ah, but there was sad news, too. Second Aunt also told me that one day a swarm of tornadoes twisted by and blew Second Uncle and his sawmill clean away. After that, in that tree full of cherries, a bald old buzzard appeared, and every day now he hums and buzzes with the bees, and carries cherry pits hither and thither, so more new cherry trees will grow."

"Dear Second Uncle!" said Brother.

"What news of my eldest brother?" asked Mama.

"Good news," said the peddler. "I saw him next, at his clearing in the woods—him and a large, happy family of pigs. And now there were apple trees again, and much new life in the woods."

"How did that happen?" asked Papa.

"You see, one winter day, an apple tree grew by a trail near Eldest Uncle's cabin. Next morning the tree was gone, but soon after that, another tree took its place, with apples on every branch. And with it, spring and summer returned, and Uncle and pigs go hunting for truffles."

"Strange," said Mama. "More magic trees."

Again, the peddler, Brother, and Sister just smiled.

"And how is Eldest Aunt?" asked Sister.

"Well, there's the sad part again," said the peddler. "A blizzard rolled in one winter, and that's the last anyone saw of her. But now, up in that apple tree, an old crow tries her best to sing with the rest of the birds. And each day, she carries apple seeds yonder and yon, and drops them where new trees can grow."

"Dear Eldest Aunt!" said Sister.

"Yes," said the peddler. "And truffles are tasty with honey. Don't you think so, cook? You know, I don't feel the least bit seasick anymore. I could eat a good meal like that."

This ought to have pleased the cook, who had been listening all this time. But all he said was, "I could cook you something special if I ever got off this ship."

"Wait," said Mama. "What about Granny?"

The peddler sighed. "I went up to Granny's as well," he said. "Of course, Granny is gone. All I found was her empty house, a nanny goat chewing on thistles, and chickens laying eggs in the weeds. After that, I walked back to town and decided to take a long vacation, to see how it felt to be rich. But all I've felt since then is seasick!"

"We must go back to the Granny's," said Mama.

"Yes," Brother and Sister agreed.

"I can't allow that," said the captain. "As captain, I must remind you four that you are still only members of my crew. The parents must go back to the bilge. The children must return to washing dishes for twelve more years."

"Twelve years?" cried the parents. "But they will be grown by then!"

"Captain," said the peddler, "there must be some reward for the people who gave you that beautiful song. There must be some reward for people who fill us with hope."

"Yes," said the cook. "And for those of us who feed you, too."

"Perhaps," said the captain, "but on board any *Wild Hope*, the stowaways must work or pay."

"Mama, Papa, why did you stow away?" asked Brother, with tears in his eyes.

"We will tell you why," said Papa. "As soon as we got off the ship, in order to earn our tickets home, we went back to working as gardener and maid, but our pay was almost nothing."

"Then what about the pigs?" asked Sister. "Why didn't you teach them to dance and make a lot of money that way?"

"Well," said Mama, "those piglets were mighty frisky. Besides, they were taking years to grow, and neither wanted dancing lessons, and neither would listen to Papa. They just wanted to play all day, and so we freed them."

"We, too, we freed piglets," said Brother.

"Then," said Papa, "*The Wild Hope* returned, heading home, and since we still couldn't pay the fare, we tried to sneak back on as stowaways and we were caught."

"We, too," said Sister.

"And for that, we were put to work in the bilge," said Papa.

"We, too," said Brother, "but washing dishes in the galley."

"Washing my dishes?" said the peddler. "I had no idea! But what can I do for you now, for everything you have done for me?"

"Nothing," said Brother, "unless you can wipe away the next twelve years."

"Easy," said the peddler. From under his bed, he pulled out a suitcase filled with money. "Captain, how much does this family owe? Because once together, never apart, they are getting off with me!"

"We're getting off!" cried Mama, Papa, Brother, and Sister.

The peddler turned to the cook and said, "And I hope *you're* getting off, too. Wouldn't you like to cook only for me?"

"Sir," replied the cook, "you will love my apple and cherry pies!"

CHAPTER TEN

Home to the Mountain

Once together, never apart.

The Wild Hope dropped them off on an island, where the peddler bought a house on a beach. The cook made the meals, and everyone took turns washing dishes until another ship arrived that would take the family home. The peddler bought them first-class tickets, so they would have a cabin on the ship.

"Good-bye," they told the peddler and cook when they left.

"Don't say that," said the cook. "Say, 'Once together, never apart.'"

The family sailed home. There, Brother and Sister ran down the gangway and searched the dock for signs of Porcabella and Mudworth, but all they found were old bits of string.

"Maybe the corn boy knows where they went," said Brother.

He asked a baggage man if the corn boy still sold snacks on the dock.

"Haven't seen him lately," said the man. "He must have gone to sea by now. He must be out there somewhere—washing dishes or pumping a bilge."

Sister was sad that the corn boy was gone, and sad to think of him working all day long as she and Brother had done. Brother also was sad. Really, he would not have minded having the corn boy as a friend.

All during the voyage, Mama had wondered what had become of her youngest brother, Youngest Uncle. The children had told her all about how Uncle had stolen them years ago, so of course Mama was angry with him. Still, she wanted to see him again.

Out the market street, the last bits of winter snow were melting. Small purple and yellow flowers squeezed up between the cobbled stones.

The family came to Broken-Heart's door. They knocked, but no one answered. The door was unlocked, so they went inside, but there was no one in the house.

"There's an orphan house around the corner," said Sister. "Uncle wanted to send us there before he decided to take us in. Maybe he came back and looked for us there, and maybe the girl has news about him."

On the orphan house gate was a padlock and a sign that said the orphan house was closed. Papa pointed to weeds that were growing in the path behind the gate.

"I think no one has lived here for months," he said.

Brother was sad that the orphan girl was gone. Sister was sad as well. Now, she would not have minded a friend like the braided girl.

They went back to Broken-Heart's house.

"We can sleep here tonight," said Papa. "In the morning, we can set out for the mountain."

Upstairs, Brother and Sister found the beds that Uncle had made them.

"So small!" said Brother, for by now they had outgrown the beds.

Here and there, they saw shavings that they had cut from the logs. They missed Porcabella and Mudworth. They missed their uncle, too. Mama and Papa shared their sadness.

"Let's not stay here," said Mama. "Let's walk out of town and sleep on the hill. The evening is warm, and the moon will be out, and tomorrow morning we will already be on our way to the mountain."

So the family left the house. On their way out of town, they bought some bread and cheese for supper, and a blanket to share.

They set off together up the hill. It had been years since Mama and Papa had hiked, so they tired faster than Brother and Sister.

"Really," Papa kept saying, "I'm so stiff from this walk already, I think my legs are made of wood. But why that should be, I do not know."

"I, too," said Mama. "I feel strange about these arms and legs. It's as though for a while I was someone or something else, but I can't remember what."

Brother and Sister winked at each other and smiled.

They were still a short way from the top when Mama spread the blanket on a patch of grass.

"We'll stay here for the night," she said.

"We're not tired," said Brother and Sister.

"Maybe not, but we are," Papa replied. "Sit down and eat before we sleep."

Brother and Sister built a fire to toast their bread and cheese. Darkness fell. As the fire died, the moon began to rise. As it did, they had all heard a rustle in the bushes.

Papa frowned.

"What's that?" Mama whispered.

"Something wild!" he said. "Quick, everyone under the blanket!"

They scrambled under the blanket and lay as quietly as they could. Sticks cracked as some big creature tromped through the bushes nearby.

"Ho," said a voice. "What's this lump in the trail?"

"I know that voice," whispered Mama.

"So do we," said Sister and Brother.

"And I know yours," said the voice.

Mama lifted the blanket. There was Uncle Broken-Heart, smiling in the moonlight.

"Brother!" Mama cried. She leaped up and folded Broken-Heart in her arms.

"Mama," said Brother, "we thought you were angry with him. Why are you hugging him now?"

"Because he's my brother!" said Mama. "But, yes, I am angry. Very!"

"You should be," Broken-Heart replied. "I need much forgiving. But first...." He let go of Mama and wrapped his arms around Sister and Brother, saying, "So you found them."

"Yes, and they found us."

Now someone else came through the bushes—a woman, tall and beautiful, with a basket balanced on her head.

"Have you met the orphan house woman?" asked Broken-Heart.

"Yes, Uncle, we have."

Broken-Heart took the woman's hand and said, "Well, we have joined together to form a family of our own. Now she is your youngest aunt."

"Who's there, Papa?" said another voice.

Out from the bushes came two more shadows.

"Braided girl!" said Brother.

"Corn boy!" Sister cried. "Oh, but is that really your name?"

"Never mind names," said the boy. "We just call each other Brother and Sister."

"We do," said the girl, "but call us cousins, which is what we call you now."

"Cousins!" said Brother and Sister.

"I'm confused," said Papa. "What are all these people doing here?"

Broken-Heart gave Papa a hug and said, "Brother-in-law, remember years and years ago, the night I boarded the ship with you?"

"No need to go over all that," said Mama. "The children have told us the terrible thing you did."

"What they say is true," said Broken-Heart. "And many years later I carved your faces for Brother and Sister. Then I felt so ashamed that I ran away. When I came back, Sister and Brother were gone. My house felt so empty without them, I went to the orphan house hoping to find them. There, a young girl told me they'd gone to the dock with their parents. 'Their parents!' I thought. So I went to the dock, where this corn boy told me how Brother and Sister had dashed alone aboard the ship. The corn boy had nowhere to go, so I brought him home for supper. That evening I went back to the orphan house, and then and there I finally learned what it means to fall in love. Since then, my sweet wife, daughter, son, and I have been waiting for you to return."

"But today," said the corn boy, "we heard there was something amazing to see from the top of this hill."

"So our parents gave us the day off from school," the girl added. "We fixed a picnic and came up here to see."

"Smell the air," said Youngest Aunt. "So sweet with flowers! We've been hearing the bees all day. And smell this, too."

She took the basket down from her head and opened it for everyone to stick their noses in.

"Honey and truffles!" said Mama.

Youngest Uncle gathered his family around him. Then he dropped to his knees and said, "Sister, forgive me. I really did try to help your children find you."

"Yes," Brother and Sister agreed. "Dear Uncle did all he could."

Mama didn't answer right away. She still felt it was an awful thing that Broken-Heart had done, taking her children away from her for all those years.

At last she said, "Words of sorrow are never enough if there are also things you can do to make life better again."

"But what else can I do?" Broken-Heart replied. "You see we each have our own lives now—you with your family and I with mine."

Mama nodded. "That is true. And at the same time—once together and never apart—we are still in each other's hearts. So promise me this, dear Brother. Promise you will give all the care and wisdom you can to these two brave children of your own. And give them all the love you can."

"I promise," he replied.

That was good enough for Mama. She drew her brother up off his knees and hugged him tightly.

Papa sniffed the wind and said, "I bet there's lots more truffles, back in the woods near Granny's mountain."

"And that's where we're going," said Brother, eagerly.

"Let's go, too!" said the cousins.

But Youngest Aunt shook her head. "You have school tomorrow," she said.

"School?" said Mama.

"Yes, there's a school in town. There isn't any on the mountain."

"Oh dear," said Mama.

"The mountain! The mountain! All go to the mountain!" Brother, Sister, and the cousins chanted.

But Youngest Uncle said, "No. Our life is in town. So we must say good-bye."

"Not good-bye," said Brother and Sister. "Once together, never apart. And good-night, cousins."

"Good-night."

Broken-Heart and his family stepped away and melted into the moonlight.

"Mama, braid my hair," said Sister.

"Of course," said Mama. She and Sister settled down. Then Mama sighed and said, "No, we can't go to Granny's. Children, you need to be in school."

"We don't!" they replied.

"You must," said Papa. "Everyone needs to learn how to read."

"Uncle taught us how to read," said Brother.

"Really?" Mama finished braiding and folded her arms. "Very well. Tell us one word you can read."

"'Closed.'"

"And where did you read it"

"Well," said Brother, "we read it earlier this evening—on a sign on the orphan house gate."

"Good!" said Papa. "But what about numbers?"

"Oh, the cook taught us numbers," said Sister. "Watch."

She lifted a hand above her head. With the tip of a finger she drew three lines against the moon. The first line was straight, and the second was straight, and the third was like part of a circle.

"What's that?" asked Mama.

Brother laughed. "Oh Mama, that's a 5!"

Papa laughed. "So, they know their numbers, too. It's clear that they don't need school. Or not right now, at least. And if they ever do, we can start one on the mountain."

"Yes," Sister agreed. "And our school will also teach pigs to dance."

"Perhaps," said Mama. "Now go to sleep, before I change my mind."

They were nearly asleep when Brother sat up and said, "Papa, can you really teach a pig to dance?"

Papa grinned and said, "Son, I can teach a crocodile to cakewalk."

"But what about pigs?"

"Well, I could try," said Papa. "But we set the piglets free. Now sleep."

Brother lay back down.

Then Sister sat up.

"We could walk all night," she said.

"No!" said the parents.

"Then can Brother and I get up and take a few more steps, to the top of the hill? Our boy-cousin said there was something amazing to see from there."

"Very well, but come right back."

Sister and Brother got up. They climbed to the top of the hill and came back down to their dozing parents.

"Papa, Mama!"

The parents yawned. "What now?"

"Come see what we saw from the top!"

"We're tired!"

"But there's snow," said Brother, "all the way from here to the mountain."

"No, dears, that's just Mother Earth in the moonlight."

"It isn't. We've seen moonlight before."

The parents began to snore, so Brother and Sister went back up the hill and returned a short while later. Soon, Papa and Mama were wakened by the gentle fall of flakes on their cheeks.

"It's snowing," mumbled Papa. He sniffed at the flakes. "But I never smelled snow so sweet." He raised his hand to his cheek. "Hmm, these snowflakes are warm," he said.

Mama touched her cheek.

"Petals," she said.

They sat up and rubbed their eyes. The children's arms were full of blossoms, white and pink in the moonlight.

"Everywhere beyond the hill," said Sister, "the land is covered with these."

Mama's eyes lit up. "Apples and cherries in bloom."

"Yes, Mama, all the way to Granny's."

"And that's where we'll head tomorrow," said Papa. "Now, sleep."

Brother and Sister lay down once more.

"Sing us to sleep," they said.

So Mama sat up again to sing.

Earth turn
Breeze blow
Brave seeds
Wind sow

Take me
With you—

"Stop!" whispered Papa. "More sounds in the bushes. Quick, everyone down!"

He pulled the blanket over their heads.

"No," said Brother. "It sounds—"

"It sounds like squeals!" said Sister.

Two small, squealing creatures ran out on the path. They dashed toward the top of the hill as fast as short, pink legs could go. Sister jumped up.

"Piglets! Mudworth!"

She ran off behind them.

"Porcabella!"

Brother jumped up, too, and raced away.

"Wait!" cried Mama.

The parents stumbled onto their feet. They grabbed the blanket and ran off in the moonlight, chasing the pigs and their runaway children.

THE END

Acknowledgements

*For ongoing support, continuing thanks to Tamim Ansary and
San Francisco Writers' Workshop; and to Anne Brodzky, Tony Williams,
and The Society for Art Publications of the Americas. Thanks also to
Donna Linden for wisdom and advice.*

Alan Venable grew up in Pittsburgh and has written many books for children and young adult readers. Among his plays are school and theatre dramatizations of this book. He lives with his wife Gail in San Francisco. Their daughter Noe is a songwriter. Their son Morgan is a product design engineer.

Laurie Marshall also grew up in Pittsburgh. She paints, writes, and educates to clarify what's important, strengthen community, and connect with the Creator. She has made many murals and dramas with young people and used art and story-telling to build consensus and prevent conflict among people of all ages. Her writings and performance works include *Stories from the Dust in the Corner.* She is the proud mother of two sons, Jeremy and Daniel Slack. She lives with her partner, Tom West, in Novato, California. See more of her art at SoulEmporium.com.

One Monkey Books is a 21st century publisher of imaginative books and plays that encourage children's interest in people and our natural environment. Forthcoming titles include a picture book series devoted to the adventures of Dr. Peanut—peanutri-cian, scientist, good neighbor, and winner of the Nobel Prize.